NICKELODEON

SpongeBob® SquarePants

Show the Bunny!

by Steven Banks
illustrated by C.H. Greenblatt and William Reiss

Ready-to-Read

Simon Spotlight/Nickelodeon

New York   London   Toronto   Sydney   Singapore

Stephen Hillenburg

Based on the TV series *SpongeBob SquarePants*® created by Stephen Hillenburg
as seen on Nickelodeon®

SIMON SPOTLIGHT
An imprint of Simon & Schuster Children's Publishing Division
1230 Avenue of the Americas, New York, New York 10020

Manufactured in the United States of America

12 14 16 18 20 19 17 15 13

Library of Congress Cataloging-in-Publication Data
Banks, Steven.
Show me the bunny! / by Steven Banks.— 1st ed.
p. cm. — (SpongeBob SquarePants ready-to-read ; #3)
"Based on the TV series SpongeBob SquarePants® created by Stephen Hillenburg as seen on Nickelodeon®."
Summary: When Patrick scares away the Easter Bunny by mistake, SpongeBob decides to put on a bunny suit and hide eggs, and Patrick finds the biggest egg either one has ever seen.
ISBN 978-0-689-86485-8
1210 LAK
[1. Easter eggs—Fiction. 2. Marine animals—Fiction.] I. Hillenburg, Stephen. II. SpongeBob SquarePants (Television program) III. Title. IV. Series.
PZ7.B22637Sh 2004   [E]—dc21   2003005850

Knock! Knock!

"Who's there?" asked Patrick.

"It's me, SpongeBob! Guess what?
    The Easter Bunny is coming tomorrow!"

Patrick jumped up and down. "Oh, boy, the Easter Bunny! Is he going to come down the chimney and bring me presents?"

PUT GIFTS HERE!

SpongeBob shook his head.
"No, Patrick. That's Santa Claus.
The Easter Bunny hides eggs and
we find them."

Patrick ran to his refrigerator and
grabbed a carton of eggs.
"I found the Easter eggs!" he shouted.
"Easter is tomorrow," said SpongeBob.
"Besides, Easter eggs are
painted pretty colors."

That night Patrick hung a stocking above his fireplace and went to bed early. SpongeBob was so excited for Easter that he counted eggs until he fell asleep.

Early the next morning the
Easter Bunny arrived and began
hiding eggs. He was about to put the
first one under Patrick's rock when
the noise stirred Patrick out of his
deep sleep.

"Ahhhhh!" screamed Patrick. "Go away,
you big, cute, fluffy monster!"
The Easter Bunny was so scared
that he swam away without leaving
any eggs! Patrick returned to bed,
proud of himself for scaring
the monster away.

Whirrr! SpongeBob's alarm clock woke him up. "I have to go get Patrick! It's time for the egg hunt!"

Patrick proudly told SpongeBob how
he saved Bikini Bottom from being
attacked by a giant monster.

When Patrick described the "monster,"
SpongeBob said, "Oh, no, you scared
away the Easter Bunny!"
Patrick began to cry.
"I ruined Easter!"

SpongeBob asked Gary what to do.
"Meow!" replied Gary.
"You are right! I will color eggs
and hide them so Patrick's Easter
will not be ruined!" said SpongeBob.

"Patrick will never know it's me
in this Easter Bunny costume,"
SpongeBob said with a giggle.

Then he darted around, hiding
Easter eggs everywhere.
"I will put one here and here and
here and here!" cried SpongeBob.

15

Squidward stuck his head out of the window and said, "SpongeBob! What are you doing?"

"I am the Easter Bunny!" SpongeBob replied.

Squidward rolled his eyes. "Right, and I am Little Red Riding Hood!"

"You are?" asked SpongeBob, amazed.
"No!" shouted Squidward. "Just be
quiet! I am trying to sleep!"

When SpongeBob was done
he knocked on Patrick's rock.
Patrick looked outside and cried,
"Merry Christmas, Easter Bunny!"

"You mean 'Happy Easter,' Patrick,"
    said SpongeBob, correcting him.
"Okay then, 'Happy Easter, Patrick!'"
    repeated Patrick.
"Never mind," said SpongeBob. "It's
    time to get your best friend and
    go on an egg hunt."

SpongeBob ran home and took off his costume. Suddenly Patrick burst in. "SpongeBob, the Easter Bunny came! I am going to win the egg hunt—I can feel it!"

"It's not a contest, Patrick," said
   SpongeBob. "We just find the eggs
   and then eat them."
Patrick ran out the door. "I am
   going to win!" he yelled.

SpongeBob and Patrick began hunting
for Easter eggs.
Soon SpongeBob's basket was full,
but Patrick could not even find
the eggs right in front of him!

23

SpongeBob secretly put some of his
eggs into Patrick's basket.
"Look! I found some eggs in my
basket!" cried Patrick happily.
"Now we both have eggs,"
said SpongeBob.

"Boy, all this work sure has made me hungry!" said Patrick.

He then ate all the eggs in his basket. As soon as they were gone he began to cry. "All my eggs are gone! I lost the contest! This is the worst Easter ever!"

SpongeBob felt sorry for Patrick.
"You can have some of my eggs."
Patrick smiled. "Really?"
"Sure," said SpongeBob.
Patrick took *all* of SpongeBob's eggs
and ran home shouting, "I have the
most eggs! I win!"

SpongeBob went home and cried.
"Gary, I gave all of our eggs away!
That means no egg sandwiches,
no egg pancakes, and no egg creams!"
"Meow," said Gary sadly.

Just then Patrick knocked on the door.

"Go away!" cried SpongeBob. "I am not in the mood for company right now, Patrick. You took all of my Easter eggs!"

"But I brought them back," said
   Patrick. "Thanks for giving them
   to me, but I do not need them
   anymore."
"Why not?" SpongeBob asked.
"Because I found the biggest Easter
   egg ever!" said Patrick.

SpongeBob looked up at the huge egg.
"Isn't it beautiful!" cried Patrick.
"I do not think that's an Easter
egg," said SpongeBob.

Suddenly the egg began to crack
and out came . . .

... a giant fish! It began
to chase them. "Run for your life!"
yelled SpongeBob.
"Merry Christmas, Easter Fishy!"
said Patrick as they ran off
into the sunset.